FAMILY TREE

Talking Trees work with Wizards closely,
Helping them out by giving advice, mostly.
How all of these Talking Trees came to be
Is when a Wizard gets old, he becomes a Tree.

GorBees

When a Tree drops an acorn in a lake or sea,
A GorBee hatches out and swims away free.
GorBees are like BeeBees of the ocean blue,
Doing things for Sea Queens all the day through.
Each GorBee will someday grow up to be
A Sea Erf that helps a Sea Queen of Ree.

Sea Erfs

Sea Erfs help the Sea Queens get through
All of the sea work they have to do.
As Sea Erfs grow up, eventually,
Sea Queens are what they'll grow up to be.
Each Sea Erf is a Princess too,
Learning to do what Sea Queens do!

Sea Ree Queens

While Wizards take care of the land with the Trees,
The Sea Rees take care of Ree's twenty-two seas.
They're not called Wizards but it's certainly true,
They can do anything the Wizards can do.
When Sea Queens get old and their work is done,
They become Talking Trees and sit in the sun.

TO

DYLAN

2019

Look at the Size of that Long-Legged Ploot!

Written and Illustrated by

Scott E. Sutton

Action Publishing

Copyright © 1989 by Scott E. Sutton. All rights reserved. Second Edition © 2003 by Scott E. Sutton. All rights reserved. The Family of Ree™ is the trademark of Scott E. Sutton. Published by Action Publishing, LLC, P.O. Box 391, Glendale, CA 91209. ISBN 1-888045-16-7. Library of Congress Control Number: 2002116457. Printed in Hong Kong through American Book.

Chapter One
Find 'Em

"Shhhh," whispered Jeeter, "don't make any sound.
Crawl under these bushes, keep close to the ground."

"Okay," said a BeeBee, who was by Jeeter's side.
They were both in the bushes trying to hide.

It was late at night and a full moon was out
As Jeeter and BeeBee were sneaking about.

"Wait! Someone's coming," Jeeter did say.
"Over there in those bushes, they're coming this way!"

"They're out here somewhere!" a BeeBee said.
He was looking through bushes, scratching his head.

"They may," yelled another, "be farther out."
So the BeeBees kept looking in the bushes about.

As soon as the BeeBees walked off in the wood,
Jeeter and BeeBee ran as fast as they could

Out from the bushes and across to a Tree.
"We made it! We made it!" they yelled with glee.

So why were those two sneaking around,
Crawling through bushes, not making a sound?

They were all playing a popular game,
It's like hide-and-seek, but Find 'Em's its name.

It's only played very late at night
Under the glow of Ree's bright moonlight.

The way the game goes is for two Erfs or BeeBees
To sneak in a circle 'round one of Ree's Trees

While another two try to find them before
The first two sneak back to the Tree and score.

Jeeter yelled to the BeeBees way out in the Trees,
"Game's over, you two. Come back here, please."

Then from Wizard's treehouse they heard a loud CRACK!
Like the sound of wood breaking, a very large stack.

Soon after the noise the BeeBees returned.
Jeeter looked at them both, a little concerned.

"Can you BeeBees tell me what made that loud crack?"
Jeeter asked the BeeBees, who were just coming back.

"I don't know," said one, "I was up in a Tree
Behind some big branches where I couldn't see."

"Well," said the other, "I saw something scoot,
And I think that it was a Long-Legged Ploot.

"This Ploot was sooo big, I let out a hoot.
I thought, 'Look at the size of that Long-Legged Ploot!'

"Maybe he stepped on a branch from a Tree
And broke it to pieces. That's what it could be."

"Okay," said Jeeter. "That's it for tonight.
Let's all get some sleep before it's daylight."

When Jeeter finished what he had said,
He ran to the treehouse to get into bed.

Chapter Two

Ploot Dreams

In a rocking chair by the warm fireplace,
Dundee looked up with a smile on his face.

"Jeeter!" he said as the Erf came in the door.
"Hello," replied Jeeter as he walked 'cross the floor.

"What," Dundee asked, "was that loud cracking sound?"
"A Ploot," Jeeter said, "was stomping around.

"I think he stepped on a branch from a Tree,
At least that's the story a BeeBee told me.

"But I didn't see it, so I don't really know
Where this Ploot came from or where he did go."

"Hmmm," mumbled Dundee, "that doesn't seem right.
A Ploot doesn't normally wander at night.

"When we get up tomorrow we must check this out,
To find out what that noise was about."

"Sure," said Jeeter, "then I'll get back to
The wooden chest I was building for you."

You see, Wizards teach Erfs how to make things from wood,
And Jeeter's woodworking was especially good.

"Ah yes," said Dundee, "I've seen what you've done.
That chest you're building is a beautiful one."

"Thanks!" said Jeeter. "I must finish, you see,
So that I can build a nice chest for me."

"All right," laughed Dundee. "Let's go get some rest
So tomorrow we both will be feeling our best."

That night Jeeter dreamed of a Long-Legged Ploot
That was five miles high with a mile-long snoot.

His fins were floppy like the ears of a bunny.
Jeeter laughed in his sleep. He thought this was funny.

The very next morning he woke with a yawn.
His dream went KAPOOF! and the big Ploot was gone.

He went downstairs to help Dundee make
Bowls of hot cereal and BeeBerry cake.

They both ate their breakfast and went out to see
Where that Ploot had stepped on the branch from a Tree.

But when they went looking for the broken Tree limb,
What they saw instead made them both look quite grim.

Chapter Three

Hunting for Ploots

Jeeter couldn't believe what his eyes did see:
A pile of pieces where his chest used to be!

"Noooo!" moaned Jeeter. "Not my wood chest!
It took so much work. It was one of my best."

The chest he'd been building was now mostly sticks.
"It will take me hours," said Jeeter, "to fix!

"I've never seen Ploots do this kind of stuff.
They never get mad and they never get rough!"

"It may have," said Dundee, "been an accident.
We need to find out where that BeeBee went—

"The one who was out here late last night—
And make sure that he's got the story right."

    They found the BeeBee
          in just a short while
    And asked how the chest
          had become a woodpile.

    "Uhhh . . . it was like I told Jeeter,"
          the BeeBee explained.
    "A Ploot stomped through and
          that's what remained.

"I thought he stepped on a large Tree limb.
It was kind of dark, I could barely see him."

"But there was," said Jeeter, "a full moon last night.
Are you sure that you have your story all right?"

"Well, of course I do," said the angry BeeBee.
"He was the biggest Ploot I ever did see!"

"All right," said Dundee. "Now tell me, BeeBee,
Could you point out this oversized Ploot to me?"

"Um, I suppose so," the BeeBee did say.
"But what difference does it make anyway?

"Why don't we all just fix up the chest?
I'll help you repair it. I think that's what's best.

"Why run through the bushes, Trees and brooks
Hunting for Ploots like hunting for crooks?"

"Because," replied Dundee, "I want to find out
Why this big Ploot was crashing about.

"It may be an accident, I don't know.
Or something scared him. That's why we must go.

"There's something not right, so we must figure out
If there's really a problem and what it's about.

"Let's start by looking near GorBee Bay.
I saw some Ploots there yesterday."

"Mind if I join you?" said a voice from behind.
"Ploots are easy for Woodrats to find."

It was Bipp, the Woodrat, Dundee's good friend,
Who had just come walking around a bend.

"Hi, Bipp," said Dundee, "I'm glad you're here.
We have a problem with Ploots, I fear."

Dundee told him the story of what happened last night.
"Let's find them," said Bipp, "'cause something's not right."

So they hiked on down to GorBee Bay
Where Bipp found Ploot tracks right away.

They followed the tracks along the shore.
"I'm guessing," Bipp said, "there're five Ploots or more."

They climbed over rocks, walked by a big Tree,
Following Ploot tracks away from the sea.

"I'm tired," said BeeBee, "and I really should go.
My Tree will be worried about me, you know."

"We need you," said Jeeter, "to point out the Ploot
That smashed up my chest and decided to scoot."

Then Bipp climbed up to a high treetop,
So Dundee and Jeeter came to a stop.

"Ploots!" yelled Bipp. "I have them in sight!
We go up this hill to the hill on the right."

Chapter Four

Just the Facts

They climbed up the hill. It wasn't too far.
At the top Jeeter yelled, "There the Ploots are!

"Which one of you Ploots stepped on my chest?
I worked really hard. It was one of my best!"

"Oh, Jeeter," said the Wizard, "to be a good sleuth,
Never act until you've got the whole truth.

"If you want to solve problems, you must have the facts.
Let me talk with the Ploots. Sit down and relax.

"All right, BeeBee," said Dundee,
        "now can you see
The Ploot from last night?
        Which one would he be?"

The BeeBee mumbled, "Ummm, they all look the same.
And he sure didn't stop to give me his name!"

"Okay," said Dundee, "then I will find out
If last night these Ploots were running about."

He asked them questions and when he was through,
Bipp asked the Ploots a question or two.

A Ploot said to them, "We don't walk at night
Because we Ploots have bad night sight.

"BeeBee's story has us very confused.
The path by your treehouse we've never used.

"If we walked by your house we wouldn't get far.
We'd trip on the roots, the size our feet are!"

"Are there others?" asked Bipp. "Maybe a stray?"
"Just us," they said. "No others, no way."

"Humph," said Dundee. He was starting to worry.
"We're not any closer to solving this story.

"Thank you, Ploots, we'll get back to you.
"Well, Bipp," said Dundee, "now what do we do?"

"Dundee," said Jeeter, "I have to say
I don't think Ploots did this and then ran away."

"You know," said Bipp, "we could look for hints
Behind your treehouse, for Ploot footprints.

"Then we will know, and the Ploots will too,
Whether BeeBee's story is false or true."

"Great!" said Dundee. "Let's get out of here
And get home before any tracks disappear.

"But I don't see BeeBee. Where could he be?"
"Probably," said Jeeter, "back home in his Tree."

They all hurried down the hill to the bay,
Then down the beach. They ran all the way.

On their way home, along the blue sea,
They came across Sea Princess Feejee.

She was in a tide pool,
          there was lots of commotion.
She was helping a Beasty
          back to the ocean.

"Hi, Feejee," said Dundee, "what's wrong with this one?"
"He's stuck," she said, "and he weighs a ton."

So Dundee, Bipp and Jeeter, the Erf,
Helped Feejee lift Beasty back to the surf.

Back in the ocean the Beast swam away.
"Thanks," said Feejee, "it's been quite a day."

"Me, too," said Jeeter, "we're doing our best
To find who it was that ruined my chest."

Jeeter told Feejee what BeeBee had said
As they all walked to the treehouse ahead.

"Let me join you," said Feejee, "because I am curious.
Poor Jeeter, I know you must have been furious."

"I was," explained Jeeter, "but not to worry.
We'll find out what's what with this giant Ploot story."

They reached the treehouse and got to the spot
Where the Ploot broke the chest, or so they had thought.

Bipp gave the scene a close looking-over.
"Aha!" he announced. "Take a look at this clover.

"If a Ploot came through here, then there would be
Lots of big Ploot tracks, but there are none I can see.

"Yet around by the chest, what I do find
Are smaller footprints of the BeeBee kind!"

"Great Flying Floojies!" Jeeter said with surprise.
"Could it be that BeeBee's been telling us lies?

"Is that why, Dundee, you saw the search through?
Because you weren't sure if this story was true?"

"The story," said Dundee, "didn't sound right to me.
So I decided to search for the truth carefully.

"I go by a line from a book on my shelf,
'To find out what's true, go look for yourself.'

"And a lesson I learned early on in my youth:
It is harder to lie than to tell the truth."

"Hmmm," said Jeeter. "I feel really bad.
I yelled at those Ploots. I made them feel sad."

"That," said Dundee, "can happen a lot
When you think things are true and they really are not."

Close by in the bushes, not too far away,
The BeeBee had heard what Dundee did say.

The BeeBee then realized what he had done:
By telling these lies he had hurt everyone—

The Ploots, Dundee and his friend Jeeter too.
What a mess he was in! Now what could he do?

He was so upset, tears came to his eyes,
All because he had told his friends lies.

"Need help?" asked Dundee, walking up from behind.
"Looks to me," he said kindly, "like you're in a bind."

"I am," sighed BeeBee. "Don't know what to do."
"Let's start," said Dundee, "with the story that's true."

So they all gathered 'round while BeeBee explained
What really had happened, till no lies remained.

"When we were playing Find 'Em last night,
I was looking for Jeeter. He was nowhere in sight.

"Where was he hiding? What place would be best?
The best place to hide would be in his wood chest!

"So I snuck up a Tree to jump down to the place
Where the chest was, but I fell on my face

"Right on the chest, and that was the sound
You all heard last night. There was no Ploot around.

"There was wood everywhere. It was a big mess.
I didn't tell Jeeter. I was too scared, I guess.

"I told you the Ploot broke the chest that I hit,
'Cause I thought we would fix it and that would be it.

"Now the chest is still broken, my friends are all mad.
And how do I fix what I did that was bad?

"No matter your name, no matter your size,
You can't go around and tell harmful lies."

"Well, BeeBee," said Dundee, "there's no need to pout.
You've taken the first step to sorting this out.

"But just being sorry is not quite enough,
When you've made others' lives become so rough."

So Dundee told BeeBee that now he had to
Make up the damage for what he did do.

First BeeBee went to talk to the Ploots
And tell the true story right to their snoots.

He helped pick some veggies for each long-legged critter
And played with their kiddies like a Ploot baby sitter.

When the Ploots were happy as a Ploot could be,
BeeBee went to the treehouse to help Dundee.

He did chores for the Wizard that had to be done,
Like cleaning the chimney, a real dirty one.

When Dundee was happy and the chimney was neater,
Dundee said, "Now make up the damage to Jeeter.

"We'll start that part in the morning," said he.
"I'm feeling much better," said the BeeBee.

When the BeeBee went home, Jeeter said to the Wizard,
"If it had been up to me he'd be stuck in a blizzard,

"Or thrown in some mud or turned to blue,
Or into a Frog, a rock or a shoe.

"But you didn't get mad or scream or shout.
The things you are doing are helping him out."

"Of course," said Dundee. "What good would it do
To turn that BeeBee into an old shoe?"

So BeeBee helped Jeeter for a day, maybe two,
With all of his chores until they were through.

They worked very hard and rebuilt that chest.
To this day Jeeter says it is one of his best.

BeeBee told Dundee, "My work is done.
I've made up the damage to everyone.

"Telling lies about others is bad, I see,
'Cause I wouldn't want that to happen to me."

"Yes," said Dundee, "what you say is true."
"I'm glad," Jeeter said, "you weren't turned to a shoe."

"Me, too," said BeeBee, "'cause I want to grow
Up to be an Erf someday, you know!"